Hot Dog

Story by Anne Cottringer
Pictures by Katherine Walker

dingles&company

Hot Dog was a city dog. He liked the smells of the city. He liked the noise of the city. He liked the hustle and the bustle.

He was rough. He was tough. He didn't walk around at the end of a leash. Not for him, the daily run in the park. Not for him, the cute little tricks … Sit up! Shake hands! Roll over!

2

"I wag my tail for no one!" said Hot Dog to his friends, Pooch and Mooch.

"And I wag my tail for no one!" barked Pooch, who wanted to be just like Hot Dog but was a little too short and little too long.

Mooch just said, "Woof!" because he couldn't stop wagging his short, stumpy tail. It wagged all the time.

Woof!

Pooch, Mooch, and Hot Dog stuck together. They shared their bones. They kept one another warm. They licked each other's wounds. And they shared Mrs. Fortini's meatballs.

Mrs. Fortini loved Hot Dog. She loved Pooch. And she loved Mooch. She wanted to make them her pets. But they wouldn't have it. They were free and they wanted to stay that way.

"If this is a dog's life, then it's a dog's life for me!" said Hot Dog.

"Woof!" said Mooch.

"And me!" barked Pooch.

Then something happened that changed everything.

Woof!

It was a cold, wet winter morning. Mrs. Fortini was just putting out a bowl of hot meatballs for her poochy pals. Hot Dog and Mooch were waiting by her back door.

"Poochie, poochie, poo!" called Mrs. Fortini. Suddenly Pooch panted around the corner.

"Stray dog catcher!" he barked. "Run for it!"

"Stray dog catcher?" said Hot Dog. "There isn't any stray dog catcher around here!"

"Oh yes, there is!" puffed Pooch. "And here he is!"

A van screeched around the corner. A man with a mean, pointy face jumped out.

STRAY

STRAY
DOG
CATCHER

6

STRAY
DOG

"You mangy mutts! I'll get you scruffy dogs off our streets or my name isn't Mr. Snatcher, the stray dog catcher!"

Hot Dog and Pooch and Mooch ran. Snatcher ran after them.

"Run, Hot Dog! Run!" cried Mrs. Fortini.

"There is no escape from Mr. Snatcher, the stray dog catcher!" cried Snatcher.

"That's what he thinks!" barked Hot Dog. "Follow me, bow-wows! Let's show this Snatcher a few sights of the city!"

7

They streaked through a park.

They raced through the market stalls.

They darted through the traffic.

They dashed down dark alleys.

8

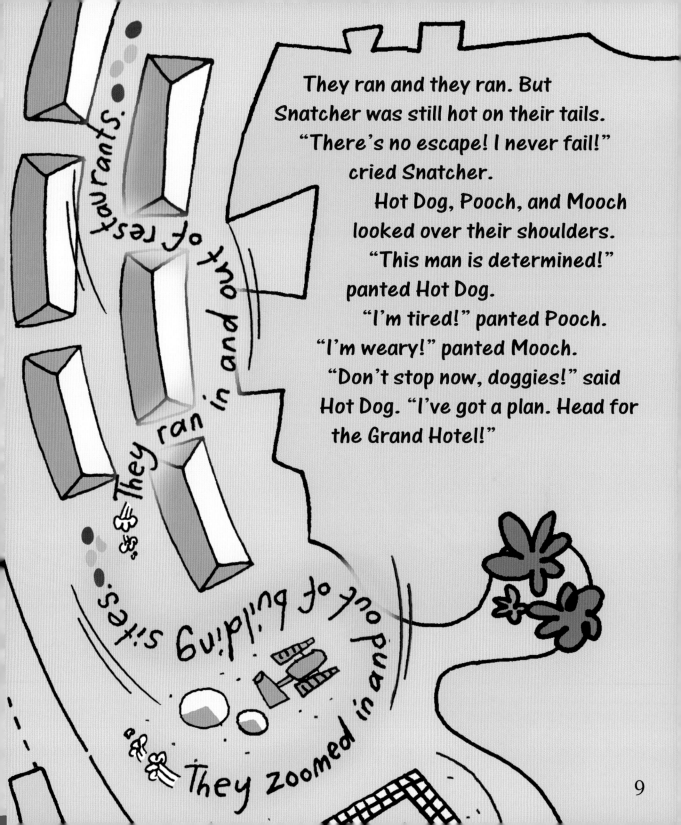

They ran and they ran. But Snatcher was still hot on their tails. "There's no escape! I never fail!" cried Snatcher.

Hot Dog, Pooch, and Mooch looked over their shoulders.

"This man is determined!" panted Hot Dog.

"I'm tired!" panted Pooch.

"I'm weary!" panted Mooch.

"Don't stop now, doggies!" said Hot Dog. "I've got a plan. Head for the Grand Hotel!"

They ran in and out of restaurants.

They ran in and out of building sites.

They zoomed in

Hot Dog bounded ahead.

Pooch and Mooch pounded behind.

"Slow down!" puffed Pooch.

"Don't stop now! We're almost there!" barked Hot Dog.

But Snatcher was about to pounce.

"Hot diggity dog! I've got you!" cried Snatcher.

"Not yet, Snatcher!" barked Hot Dog. They were almost at the door of the Grand Hotel.

"When I say 'NOW,' do what I do!" said Hot Dog.

"NOW!" barked Hot Dog. He stopped right beside a curly white poodle who was standing by the front door of the Grand Hotel. Pooch and Mooch stopped too. Hot Dog put his black nose in the air – just like the curly white poodle. He held his tail very straight in the air just like the curly white poodle.

Pooch and Mooch put their black noses in the air. They held their tails very straight in the air. (Well, Mooch tried, but his stumpy tail wouldn't go straight up in the air.)

Then they followed the curly white
poodle right through the big swinging
doors of the Grand Hotel.

Snatcher was just about to follow,
when the doorman put out his hand.

"Sorry, sir!" said the doorman.
"Guests only."

"But! But!..." spluttered Snatcher.

Hot Dog, Pooch, and Mooch trotted on.
Snatcher stood on the pavement and
spluttered some more.

"Just follow me and keep those noses in
the air," muttered Hot Dog. They trotted
through the hotel lobby, down some stairs,
along a hall, up some stairs – until they
reached a back door. All around them people
stared and leaped out of their way.

Then they trotted right out of the back door
and into an alley.

"Phew!" gasped Hot Dog. "That was
close!"

"Very close!" puffed Pooch.

"Too close!" huffed Mooch.

"And I don't think we've seen the last
of Snatcher!" said Hot Dog.

Hot Dog was right. That wasn't the last of Snatcher. The next day Snatcher chased them around the stores.

And the day after that he chased them around a fairground.

And the next day after that day, he chased them around the museum.

"I'll never give up, you horrible hounds!" he cried.

Hot Dog was getting thinner and thinner. Pooch was getting thinner and thinner. And Mooch's tail had stopped wagging. The only thing that kept them going was Mrs. Fortini's meatballs.

"My poor doggies!" she cried.
"Mr. Snatcher is a very bad man!"

"If this is a dog's life, then I would rather be a cat!" said Mooch.
"I don't think I can keep running!" said Pooch.

17

"We can't give up!" said Hot Dog. "If Snatcher catches us, we'll be in dog jail forever! There will be no more steaks from Jack's Grill. No more meatballs from Fortini's restaurant. No more bones from Bob the Butcher."

"We need a plan," said Pooch.

"A really good plan!" said Mooch.

"And I think I've got one," said Hot Dog.

"Look at that dog over there. Why doesn't Snatcher grab that dog?"

"Because its owner has it on a leash," said Pooch.

18

"Exactly!" said Hot Dog.

"But we don't have an owner. And we don't have leashes," said Mooch.

"We can get one!" cried Hot Dog.

"But we don't want one!" yelped Pooch.

"Desperate times need desperate measures!" said Hot Dog.

"What does that mean?" asked Mooch.

"It means we have to make another plan," said Hot Dog. "Now come close and listen to Hot Dog's Desperate Dog Plan, Number One-hundred-and-one."

Their plan was ready. Hot Dog, Pooch, and Mooch were just about to eat a big bone from Bob the Butcher's garbage bin, when ... Snatcher leaped out.

"Gotcha! You beastly bow-wows!"

Hot Dog barked. In a flash, Hot Dog, Pooch, and Mooch dashed down the road. Snatcher dashed down the road behind them.

"It's time to put our plan into action!" barked Hot Dog. "Fortini's is just ahead!"

"Here we come, Mrs. Fortini!" they all barked together.

Then Hot Dog, Pooch, and Mooch dived through the door of Mrs. Fortini's restaurant.

20

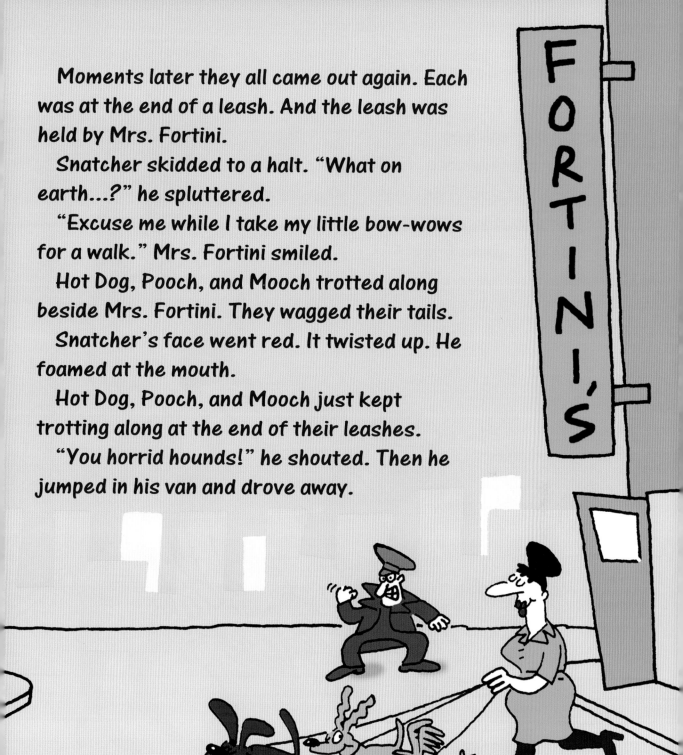

Moments later they all came out again. Each was at the end of a leash. And the leash was held by Mrs. Fortini.

Snatcher skidded to a halt. "What on earth...?" he spluttered.

"Excuse me while I take my little bow-wows for a walk." Mrs. Fortini smiled.

Hot Dog, Pooch, and Mooch trotted along beside Mrs. Fortini. They wagged their tails.

Snatcher's face went red. It twisted up. He foamed at the mouth.

Hot Dog, Pooch, and Mooch just kept trotting along at the end of their leashes.

"You horrid hounds!" he shouted. Then he jumped in his van and drove away.

FORTINI'S

21

Hot Dog, Pooch, and Mooch
barked. Mrs. Fortini laughed and
took off the leashes.
   "Your plan worked, Hot Dog! And
now I'll set you free again," she said.
"Let's just hope that Snatcher
doesn't come back."

22

That night, Mrs. Fortini gave Hot Dog, Pooch, and Mooch an extra big plate of meatballs.

"Yummy!" said Mooch, still wagging his tail.

"Scrummy!" said Pooch.

"Delicious!" said Hot Dog.

Soon there was not a meatball in sight. Mrs. Fortini came to the back door. "Finished?" she asked.

They licked their chops. They wagged their tails.

"If this is a dog's life, then it's a dog's life for me!" they said to one another, and they trotted off to look for some pudding.

24